DiNo School

Meet Teddy Rex!

by Bonnie Williams • illustrated by John Gordon

Ready-to-Read

Simon Spotlight
New York London Toronto Sydney New Delhi

SIMON SPOTLIGHT
An imprint of Simon & Schuster Children's Publishing Division
1230 Avenue of the Americas, New York, New York 10020
Copyright © 2012 Simon & Schuster, Inc.
SIMON SPOTLIGHT, READY-TO-READ, and colophon are registered trademarks of Simon & Schuster, Inc.
For information about special discounts for bulk purchases, please contact Simon & Schuster
Special Sales at 1-866-506-1949 or business@simonandschuster.com.
Manufactured in the United States of America 0612 LAK
First Edition
10 9 8 7 6 5 4 3 2 1
Library of Congress Cataloging-in-Publication Data
Williams, Bonnie.
Meet Teddy Rex! / by Bonnie Williams ; illustrated by John Gordon.
p. cm. — (Ready-to-read) (Dino School ; #1)
Summary: New student Teddy the Tyrannosuarus Rex learns to use his "inside roar" inside the classroom.
[1. Dinosaurs—Fiction. 2. First day of school—Fiction. 3. Schools—Fiction. 4. Behavior—Fiction.] I. Gordon, John, 1967- ill.
II. Title.
PZ7.W655872Te 2012
[E]—dc23
2011049207
ISBN 978-1-4424-4995-4 (pbk)
ISBN 978-1-4424-4996-1 (hc)
ISBN 978-1-4424-4997-8 (eBook)

Welcome to school—
Dino School!

"Good morning, class,"
says Ms. G.

"Please give a big Dino School welcome to our new student, Teddy the Tyrannosaurus rex."

"Hi, Teddy," says the class.

SLAM!

"Hi, everyone!" roars Teddy.

Teddy is very loud!

"I am sorry," says Teddy.

"That is okay," says Ms. G.
"Next time just use your
inside roar."

Teddy sits down at his desk. "Everyone take out a pencil and draw a picture of yourself doing your favorite thing," instructs Ms. G.

Teddy knows just what to draw.

He draws a picture of himself.

In the picture he is roaring.

"Wow, great picture!"
says Tina the Triceratops.
"You are a good artist."

"Thanks!" roars Teddy.

He is very loud again.

"I am sorry," says Teddy.

"I forgot to use my inside roar."

"I know a place where
you can roar as loudly
as you want," says Ms. G.

Ring! Ring! goes the bell.
"Time for recess!" says Bill
the Brachiosaurus.
"Follow me, everyone,"
announces Ms. G.

Outside at recess, all the
dinosaurs want to hear
Teddy roar.
"How loud is your
loudest roar?"
asks Val the Velociraptor.

"I bet you can roar louder
than thunder,"
says Pete the Pterodactyl.
"Or louder than fireworks,"
adds Steve the Stegosaurus.

Teddy looks at Ms. G.

Ms. G. nods.

"Recess is the perfect place
for your outside roar, Teddy."
she assures him.

So Teddy takes a deep breath
in . . .

and in . . .

and in. . . .

And lets out a great big . . .
ROAR!

"Hooray for Teddy!"
the students all cry.
"That was the greatest
dinosaur roar I have ever
heard!" cheers Ms. G.

Teddy smiles.

Teddy still loves to roar.
But now he knows when
to use his inside roar . . .

and when to use his
outside roar!